livin' the mermaid princess life...

Special thanks to Diane Reichenberger, Cindy Ledermann, Jocelyn Morgan, Tanya Mann, Julia Phelps, Sharon Woloszyk, Rita Lichtwardt, Carla Alford, Renee Reeser Zelnick, Rob Hudnut, David Wiebe, Shelley Dvi-Vardhana, Gabrielle Miles, Rainmaker Entertainment, Walter P. Martishius, and Sarah Lazar

Published in the United States by Golden Books, an imprint of Random House Children's Books, a division of Random House LLC, 1745 Broadway, New York, NY 10019, and in Canada by Random House of Canada Limited, Toronto, Penguin Random House Companies. No part of this book may be reproduced or copied in any form without permission from the copyright owner. Golden Books, A Golden Book, A Big Golden Book, the G colophon, and the distinctive gold spine are registered trademarks of Random House LLC.
randomhouse.com/kids
ISBN 978-0-385-37409-5
Printed in the United States of America
10 9 8 7 6 5 4 3 2 1

Barbie™
The Pearl Princess

Adapted by Kristen L. Depken

Based on the screenplay by Cydne Clark & Steve Granat

Illustrated by Ulkutay Design Group

 A GOLDEN BOOK • NEW YORK

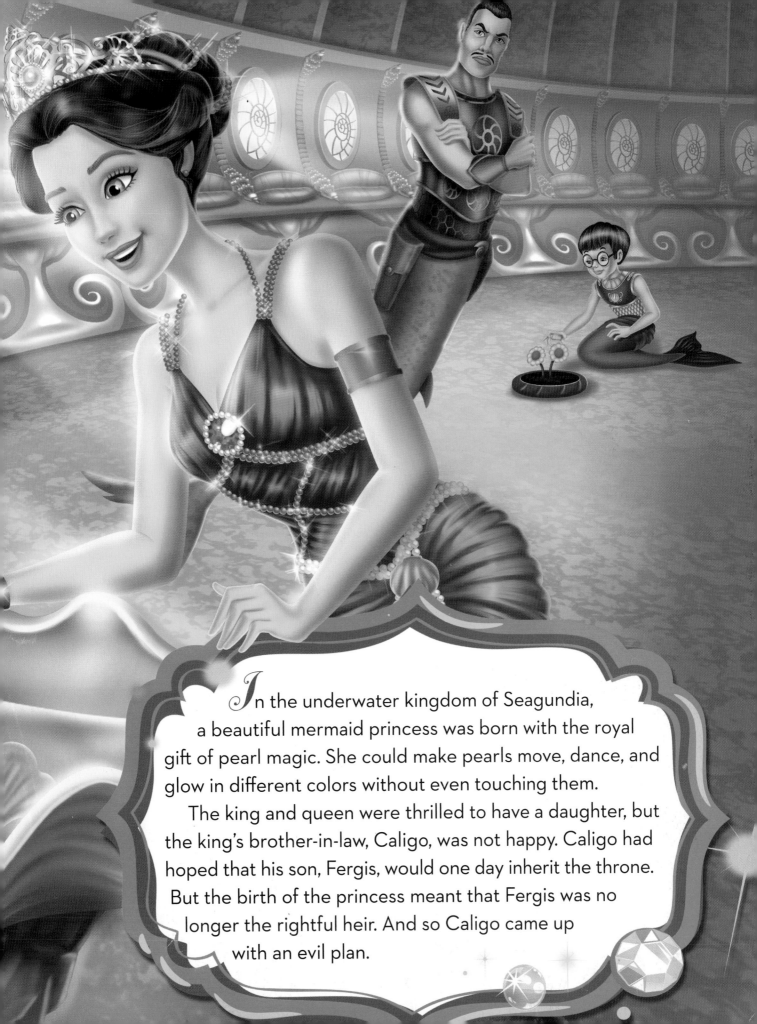

In the underwater kingdom of Seagundia, a beautiful mermaid princess was born with the royal gift of pearl magic. She could make pearls move, dance, and glow in different colors without even touching them.

The king and queen were thrilled to have a daughter, but the king's brother-in-law, Caligo, was not happy. Caligo had hoped that his son, Fergis, would one day inherit the throne. But the birth of the princess meant that Fergis was no longer the rightful heir. And so Caligo came up with an evil plan.

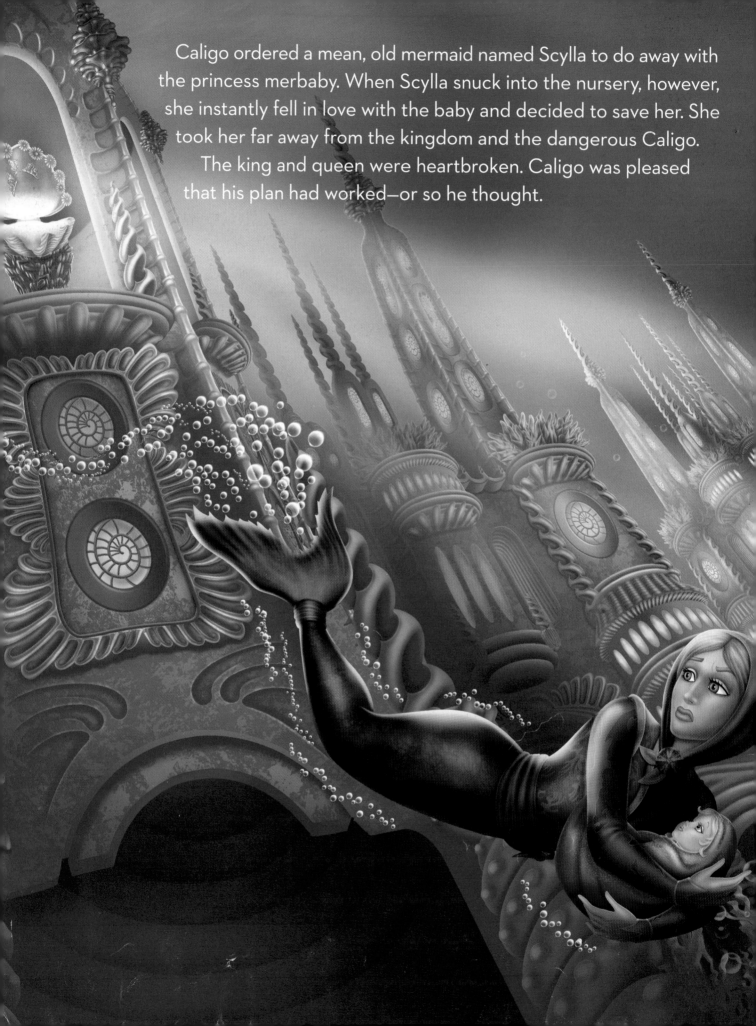

Caligo ordered a mean, old mermaid named Scylla to do away with the princess merbaby. When Scylla snuck into the nursery, however, she instantly fell in love with the baby and decided to save her. She took her far away from the kingdom and the dangerous Caligo. The king and queen were heartbroken. Caligo was pleased that his plan had worked—or so he thought.

Scylla named the merbaby Lumina and secretly raised her as
her own. Before long, the princess grew into a beautiful young
mermaid. Lumina had no idea about her past, but her pearl
powers became stronger every day. She loved creating magical
pearl hairstyles for her sea horse friend, Kuda. The two would
dress up and pretend they were royalty.

"Do you think we'll ever get to see the castle?" Lumina said
to Kuda one day.

"Maybe someday," replied Kuda.

Meanwhile, at the castle, Caligo was trying to convince the king and queen to give Fergis the Pearl of the Sea, a royal medallion that would make him the kingdom's next ruler. Caligo didn't care that Fergis was a shy young man who only dreamed of becoming a botanist.

The king and queen were hesitant, but Caligo convinced them that the kingdom was in need of an heir.

"Perhaps it *is* time," said the queen.

The king agreed. The next step of Caligo's wicked plan was in motion.

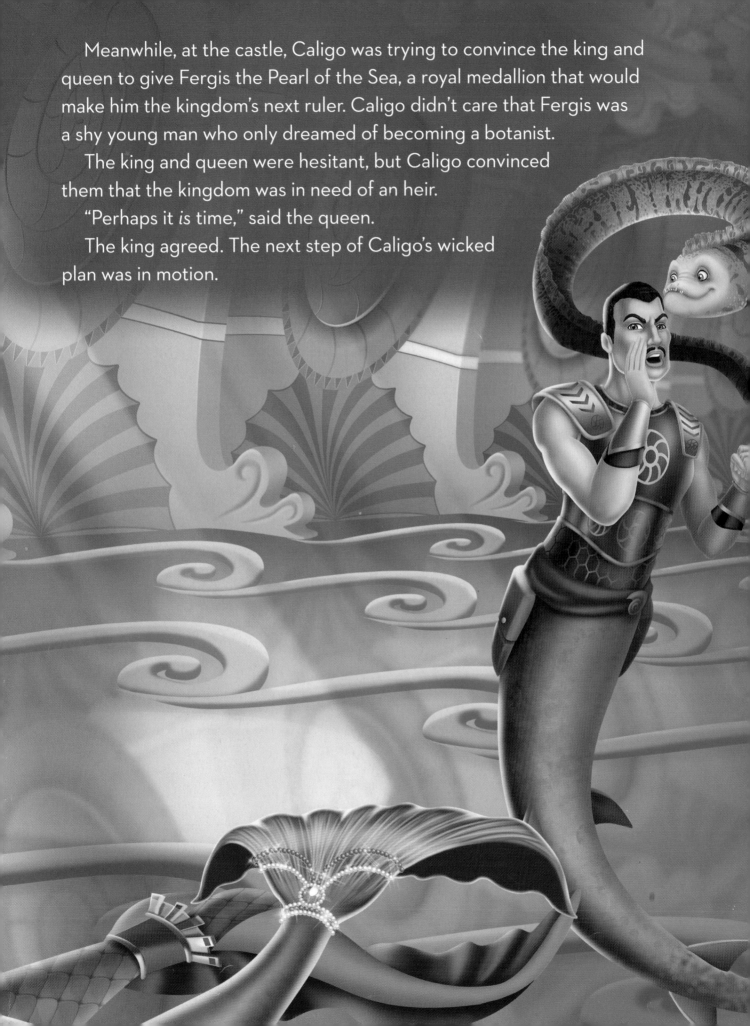

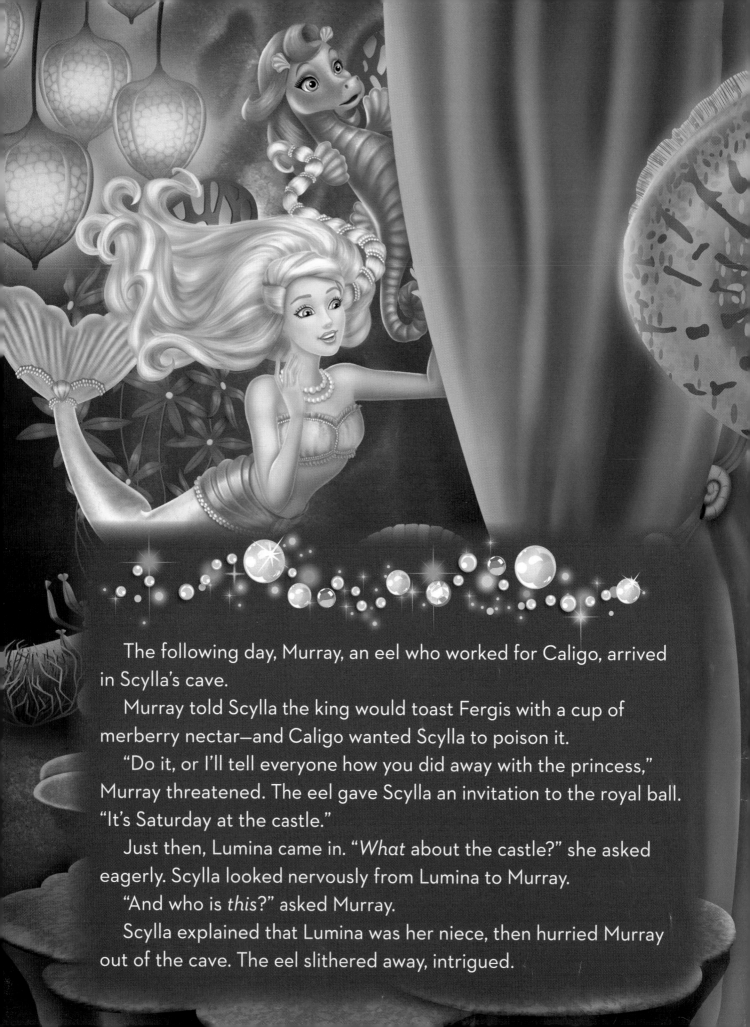

The following day, Murray, an eel who worked for Caligo, arrived in Scylla's cave.

Murray told Scylla the king would toast Fergis with a cup of merberry nectar—and Caligo wanted Scylla to poison it.

"Do it, or I'll tell everyone how you did away with the princess," Murray threatened. The eel gave Scylla an invitation to the royal ball. "It's Saturday at the castle."

Just then, Lumina came in. "*What* about the castle?" she asked eagerly. Scylla looked nervously from Lumina to Murray.

"And who is *this*?" asked Murray.

Scylla explained that Lumina was her niece, then hurried Murray out of the cave. The eel slithered away, intrigued.

"Did he mean the royal castle?" asked Lumina when Murray left.
"Are you going there? Can I go? Please?"

"Absolutely not!" replied Scylla as she packed a bag. "It's far too
risky for a young girl. I'll be back in a few days." She kissed Lumina
good-bye and headed out the door.

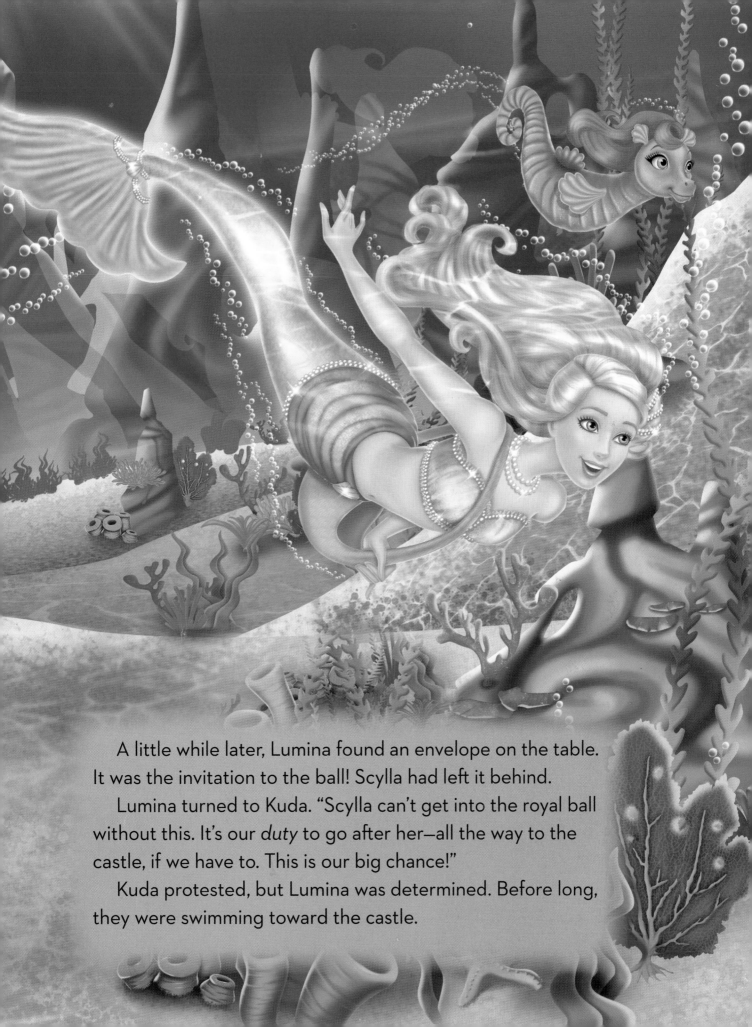

A little while later, Lumina found an envelope on the table. It was the invitation to the ball! Scylla had left it behind.

Lumina turned to Kuda. "Scylla can't get into the royal ball without this. It's our *duty* to go after her—all the way to the castle, if we have to. This is our big chance!"

Kuda protested, but Lumina was determined. Before long, they were swimming toward the castle.

Lumina and Kuda were passing through a dark kelp forest when they suddenly heard a *ROAR*!

A large, spiky fish jumped out at them. His name was Spike, and he was a stonefish.

"You'd better move it!" he warned. "Each of my poisonous spikes means a terrible, horrible end for you."

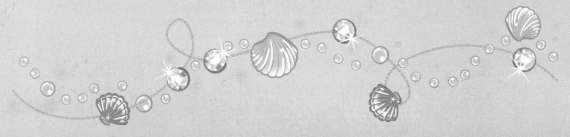

Lumina had a feeling Spike was being mean because he was lonely. She believed in leaving things better than she found them, so she quickly waved her hand. Magical pearls zipped out of a pouch she kept around her waist and landed on each of the fish's sharp spikes, making them safe.

"Now what am I supposed to do?" cried Spike sadly.

"Just be nicer," said Lumina. "Once no one's afraid of you, I bet you'll have loads of friends. We're heading to the city. There's lots of fish there. You could practice being friendly to them."

The three friends swam off together and soon spotted magnificent buildings twinkling in the distance. "The castle!" Lumina cried. They had arrived in Seagundia.

Once they got closer, they could see that the kingdom was full of skyscrapers with shiny spiral tops. Merfolk swam in all directions in the bustling city.

Suddenly, Lumina spotted Scylla crossing the street! Lumina reached into her bag for the invitation to the ball, but she couldn't find it.

"Uh-oh," she said. "I must have lost it in the kelp!"

"She'll be angry we left the reef," said Kuda. "C'mon!" She pulled Lumina into a nearby shop before Scylla could see them.

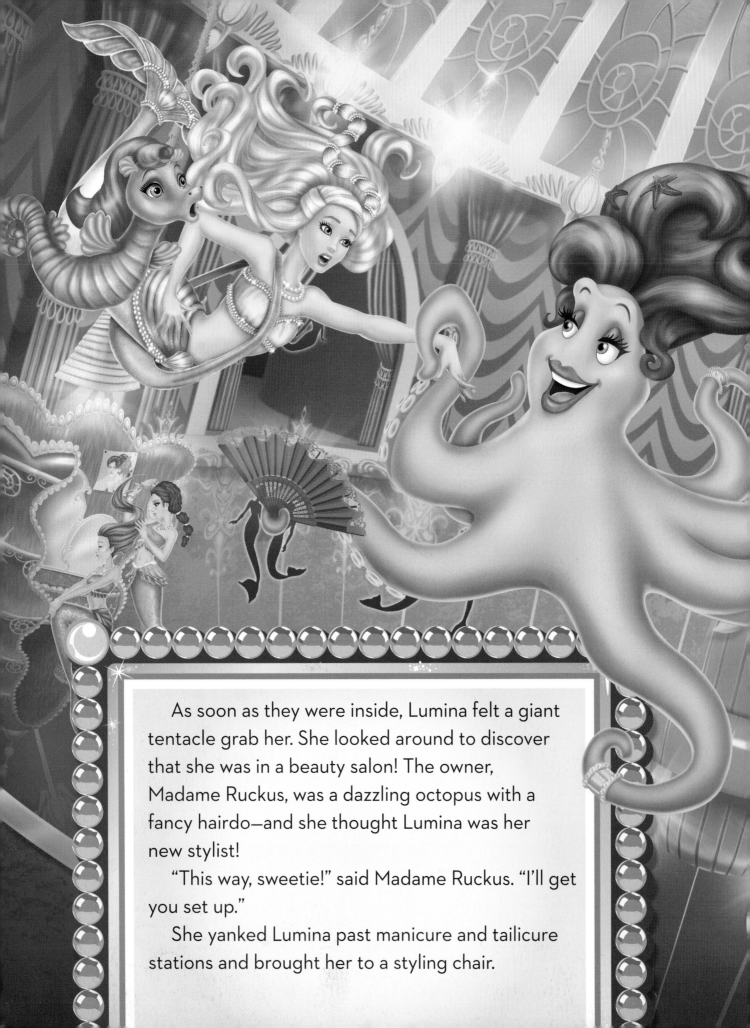

As soon as they were inside, Lumina felt a giant tentacle grab her. She looked around to discover that she was in a beauty salon! The owner, Madame Ruckus, was a dazzling octopus with a fancy hairdo—and she thought Lumina was her new stylist!

"This way, sweetie!" said Madame Ruckus. "I'll get you set up."

She yanked Lumina past manicure and tailicure stations and brought her to a styling chair.

"Here's your first customer," Madame Ruckus said. She sat a young mermaid in Lumina's chair and then whirled away to answer the phone.

Lumina didn't want to disappoint her first client. She grabbed a handful of pearls from her pouch and magically arranged them in the mergirl's hair.

"I love it!" cried the mergirl when Lumina was done.

Everyone else in the salon loved the hairdo, too, and soon they were all asking for one-of-a-kind styles. Lumina had a job!

Back at the castle, Murray told Caligo that Scylla had a niece. The eel also showed Caligo something he had found in Scylla's cave—a bracelet that had once belonged to the baby princess. Suspicious, Caligo gave Murray an order: "Find that girl!"

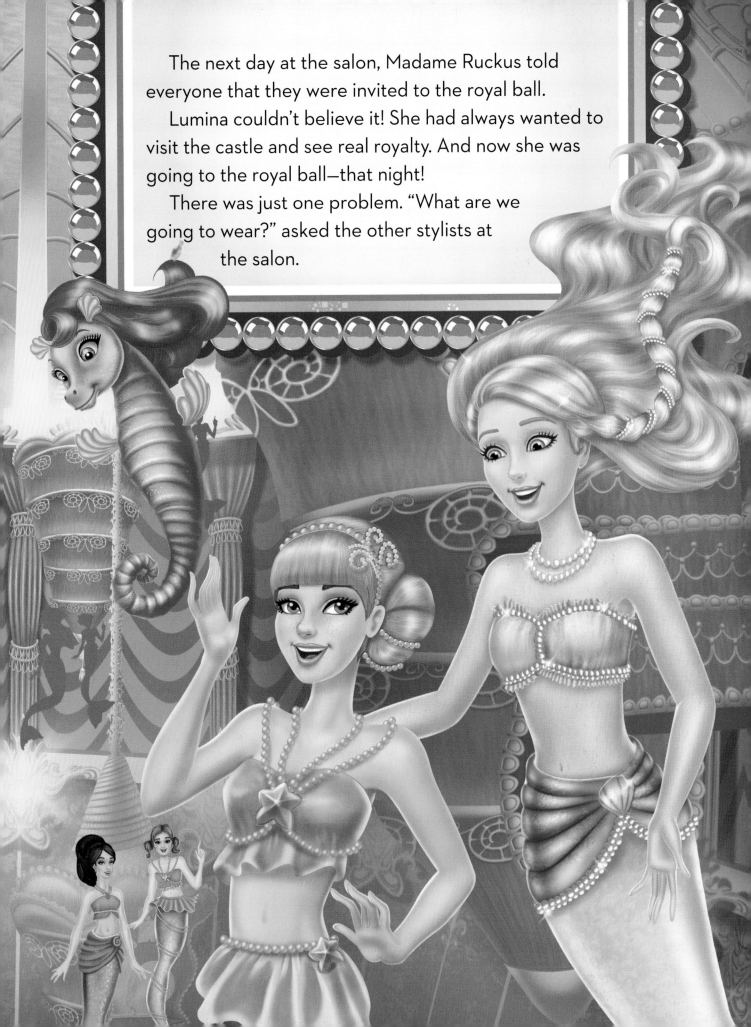

The next day at the salon, Madame Ruckus told everyone that they were invited to the royal ball.

Lumina couldn't believe it! She had always wanted to visit the castle and see real royalty. And now she was going to the royal ball—that night!

There was just one problem. "What are we going to wear?" asked the other stylists at the salon.

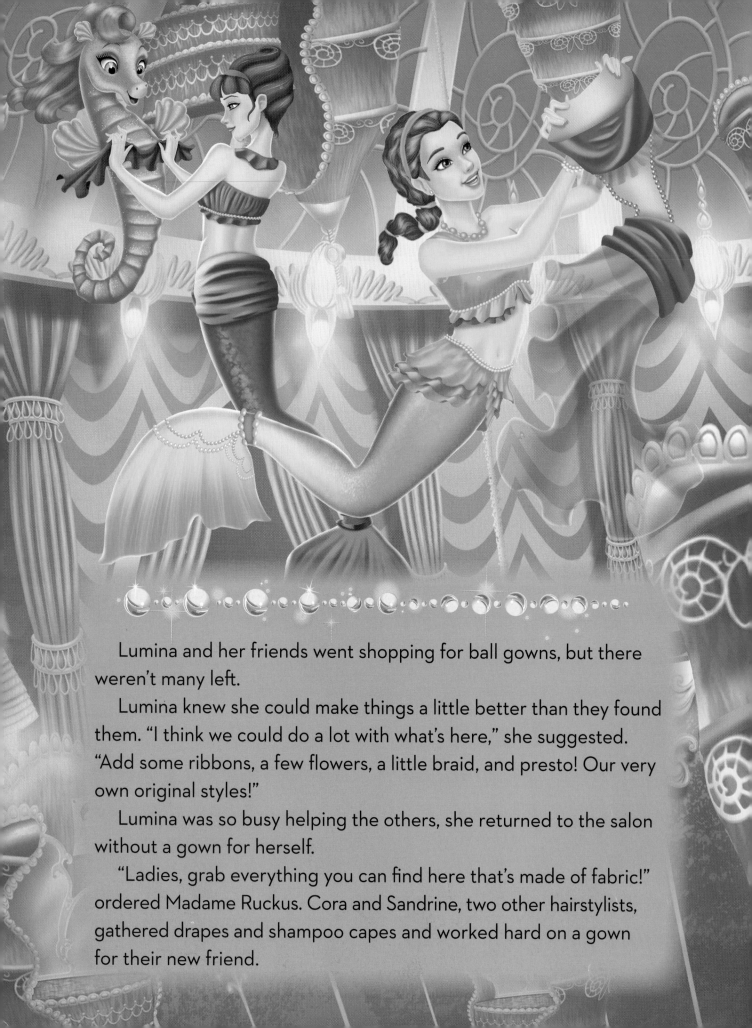

Lumina and her friends went shopping for ball gowns, but there weren't many left.

Lumina knew she could make things a little better than they found them. "I think we could do a lot with what's here," she suggested. "Add some ribbons, a few flowers, a little braid, and presto! Our very own original styles!"

Lumina was so busy helping the others, she returned to the salon without a gown for herself.

"Ladies, grab everything you can find here that's made of fabric!" ordered Madame Ruckus. Cora and Sandrine, two other hairstylists, gathered drapes and shampoo capes and worked hard on a gown for their new friend.

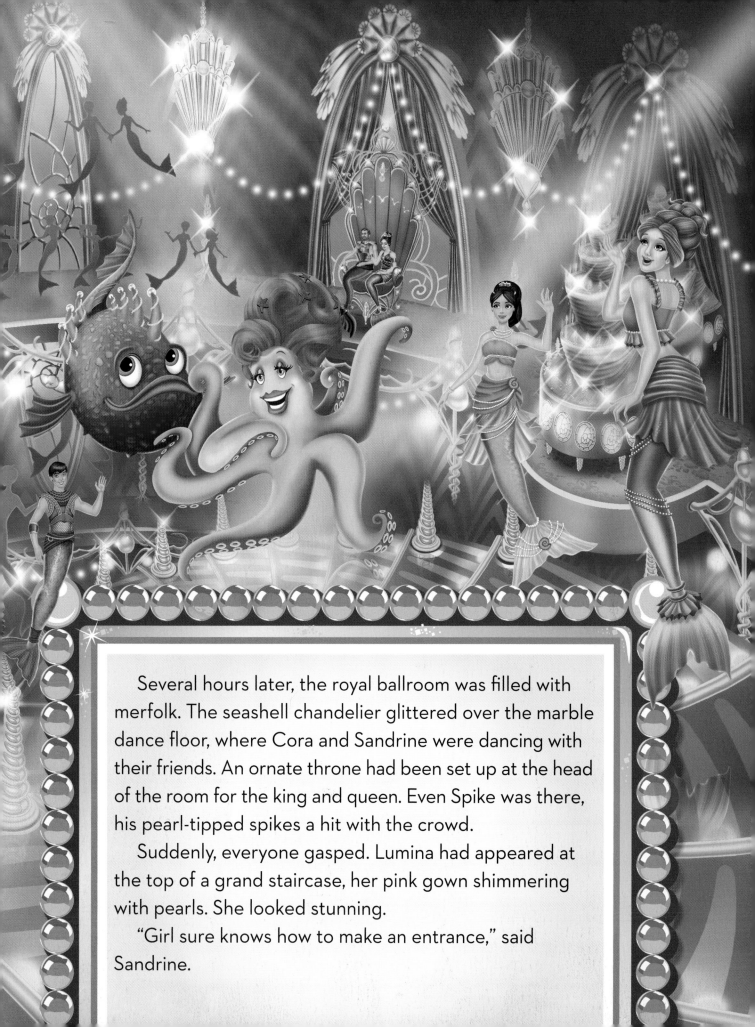

Several hours later, the royal ballroom was filled with merfolk. The seashell chandelier glittered over the marble dance floor, where Cora and Sandrine were dancing with their friends. An ornate throne had been set up at the head of the room for the king and queen. Even Spike was there, his pearl-tipped spikes a hit with the crowd.

Suddenly, everyone gasped. Lumina had appeared at the top of a grand staircase, her pink gown shimmering with pearls. She looked stunning.

"Girl sure knows how to make an entrance," said Sandrine.

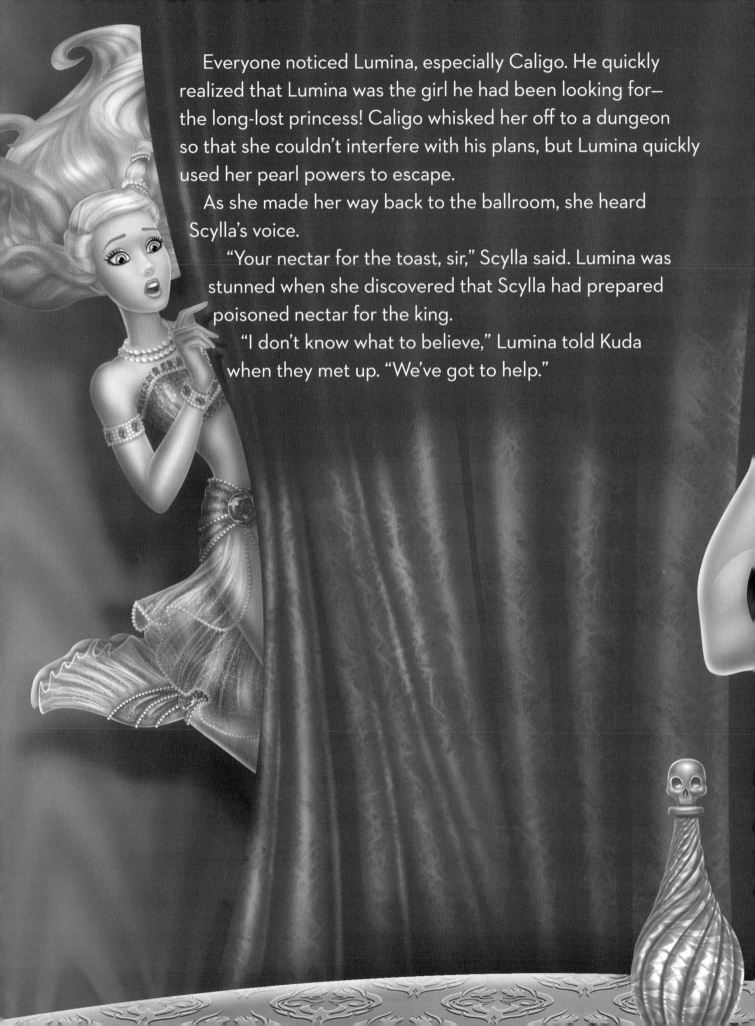

Everyone noticed Lumina, especially Caligo. He quickly realized that Lumina was the girl he had been looking for— the long-lost princess! Caligo whisked her off to a dungeon so that she couldn't interfere with his plans, but Lumina quickly used her pearl powers to escape.

As she made her way back to the ballroom, she heard Scylla's voice.

"Your nectar for the toast, sir," Scylla said. Lumina was stunned when she discovered that Scylla had prepared poisoned nectar for the king.

"I don't know what to believe," Lumina told Kuda when they met up. "We've got to help."

Moments later, the king and queen took their places on the throne.
The king presented the Pearl of the Sea to Fergis. Scylla handed the cup
of poisoned nectar to the king as he prepared to give a toast.

"To the future ruler of Seagundia!" said the king. "To Fergis!"

"No!" Scylla shouted when the king raised his cup. She rushed toward
him, but guards held her back.

Just then, Lumina burst in and knocked the cup out of the king's hand.
The crowd gasped.

"Arrest her!" Caligo ordered the guards.

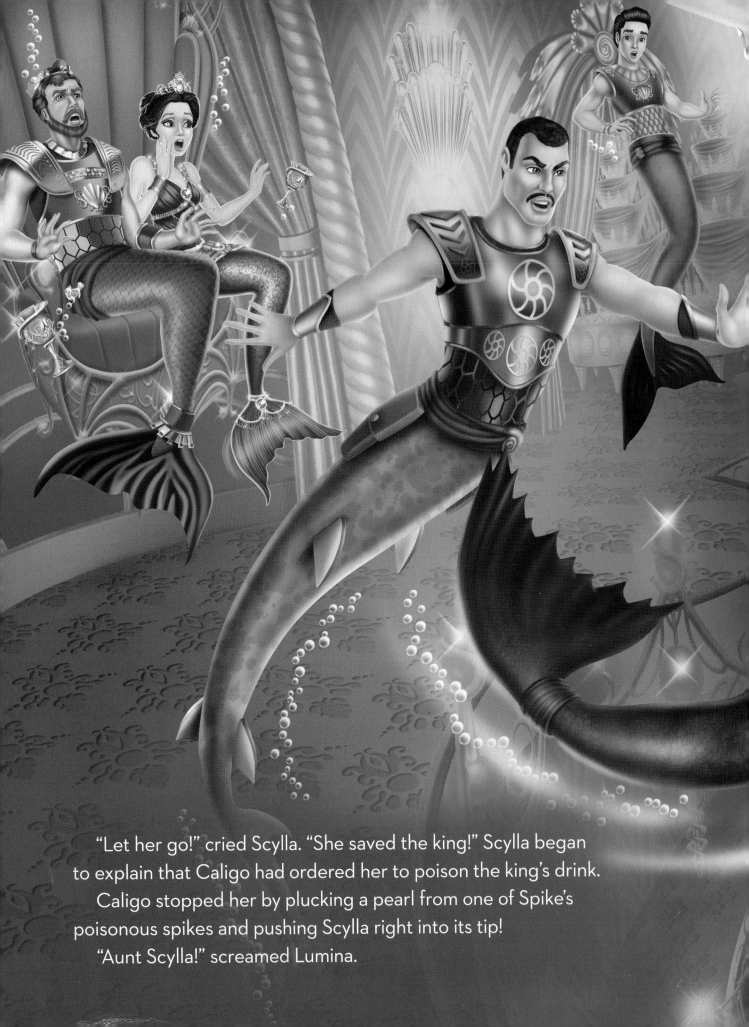

"Let her go!" cried Scylla. "She saved the king!" Scylla began
to explain that Caligo had ordered her to poison the king's drink.
Caligo stopped her by plucking a pearl from one of Spike's
poisonous spikes and pushing Scylla right into its tip!
"Aunt Scylla!" screamed Lumina.

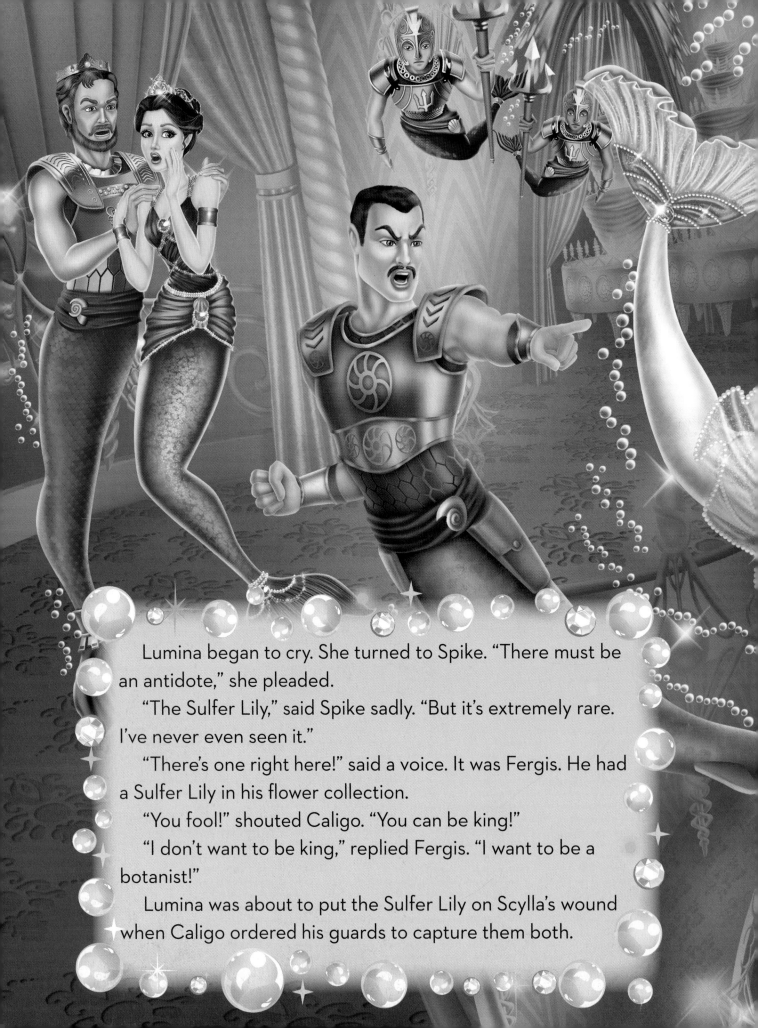

Lumina began to cry. She turned to Spike. "There must be an antidote," she pleaded.

"The Sulfer Lily," said Spike sadly. "But it's extremely rare. I've never even seen it."

"There's one right here!" said a voice. It was Fergis. He had a Sulfer Lily in his flower collection.

"You fool!" shouted Caligo. "You can be king!"

"I don't want to be king," replied Fergis. "I want to be a botanist!"

Lumina was about to put the Sulfer Lily on Scylla's wound when Caligo ordered his guards to capture them both.

"Don't you touch her!" shouted Lumina.
She closed her eyes and summoned every pearl in
the room. They whooshed through the crowd and formed
a swirling pearl tornado, stopping Caligo's guards.

As Fergis knelt down to give Scylla the Sulfer Lily petals,
the king and queen looked at each other. Lumina's pearl
powers could only mean one thing—she was their daughter.

"Aunt Scylla, please stay with me!" urged Lumina. Slowly,
the old woman's eyes began to open. She smiled at Lumina.
Then she pointed to Caligo.

"It was him," said Scylla. "He's the one who ordered me
to poison Your Majesty."

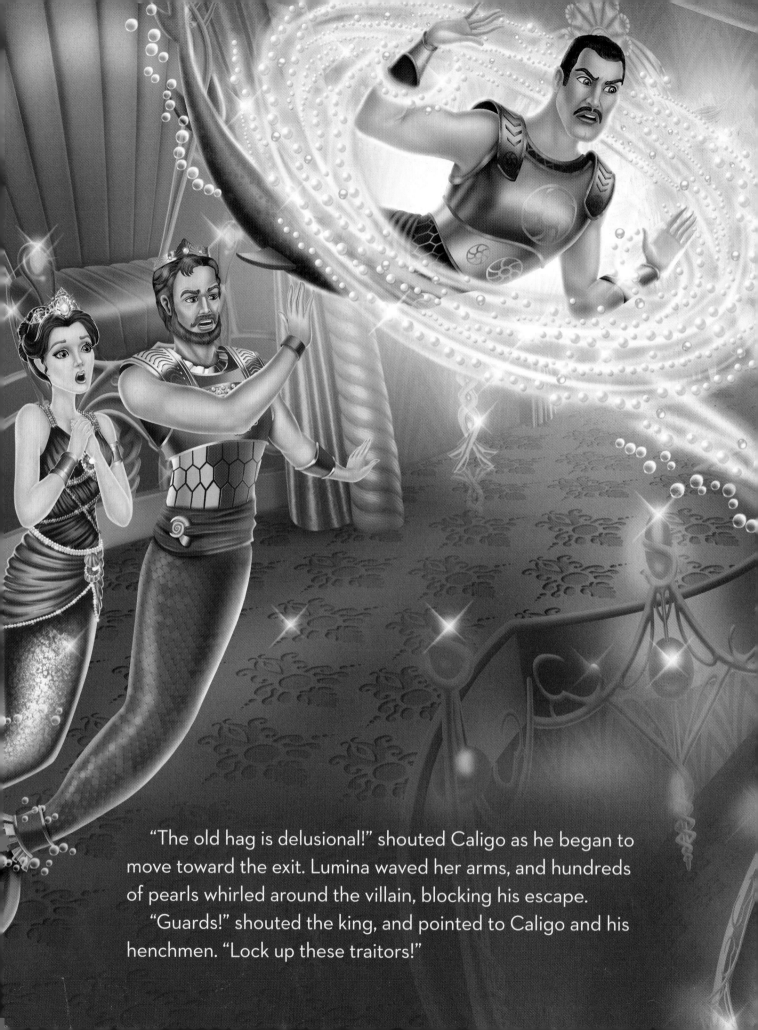

"The old hag is delusional!" shouted Caligo as he began to move toward the exit. Lumina waved her arms, and hundreds of pearls whirled around the villain, blocking his escape.

"Guards!" shouted the king, and pointed to Caligo and his henchmen. "Lock up these traitors!"

Then the king turned to Lumina. "You have the royal gift—the pearl magic!"

"Could you be our daughter?" the queen asked.

Lumina looked at them in confusion.

"She is," said Scylla. "Years ago, Caligo paid me to do away with her. But I couldn't do it. So I raised her instead—away from him. I'm so sorry."

"In that case, this belongs to Lumina," said Fergis, and he placed the Pearl of the Sea around Lumina's neck.

Lumina's tail magically glowed blue to pink, then purple to a glistening gold. Then her dress transformed into a pearlescent pink gown, and a sparkling pink tiara appeared on her head. The crowd cheered.

"Welcome home," said the king.

Lumina couldn't have been happier. She had been reunited with her mother and father and had a royal palace to live in. Scylla and Kuda could even come live with her! She felt like a princess inside and out.

"Music, please!" called the king, and the band began to play again. Princess Lumina danced the night away with her family and friends—old and new.

Max
y el Pájaro

Ed Vere

Editorial EJ Juventud

Provença, 101 – 08029 Barcelona

Este es Max.

Max es un gatito.

Los gatitos cazan pájaros.

Este es el Pájaro.

El Pájaro es un pájaro.

Los pájaros son cazados por los gatitos.

"Hola, Pájaro", dice Max. "¿Quieres ser mi amigo?".

"¡Sí, claro!", responde el Pájaro.

"Primero, te perseguiré", dice Max.

"Y luego, *quizá* te comeré.

¡Pareces un aperitivo suculento!".

"¡No me gusta ser perseguido!",
dice el Pájaro. "Y soy *demasiado*
joven para ser un aperitivo
suculento . . .

¡Ni **siquiera** he aprendido a volar! . . .".

"Oh", contesta Max, "pero es una ley de la naturaleza:
los pájaros son cazados por los gatos".

"¡Pero los amigos no se comen
entre ellos!", dice el Pájaro.

"Mmm", dice Max. "Tenemos que pensarlo".

Max y el Pájaro se sientan a pensar.

"¡Ya sé!", dice el Pájaro.

"¡Tengo una idea!".

El Pájaro le explica a Max
los principios básicos de la amistad.

"Los amigos se lo pasan bien juntos
y se ayudan el uno al otro . . .".

"Si me enseñas a volar", dice el Pájaro,

"luego podremos hablar sobre perseguirme . . .

. . . y todas esas *otras cosas,* ¿de acuerdo?".

"Esto me parece justo y razonable", dice Max.

Los dos aceptan el trato.

Max le explica al Pájaro los principios básicos del vuelo.

"Bueno, Pájaro, primero de todo,
tienes que . . . Esto . . .
Lo que tienes que . . .
Bueno . . .

. . . Ejem", carraspea Max.

"Creo que yo tampoco sé volar".

"Sígueme", dice el Pájaro. "Iremos a la biblioteca . . .".

Las bibliotecas lo saben todo.

En la biblioteca hay una sección de vuelo.

Pero Max y el Pájaro no alcanzan
los libros de la estantería de arriba . . .

. . . entonces piden en préstamo
algunos de la de abajo.

Max y el Pájaro estudian durante semanas.

Leen libros importantes
hasta que sus pequeños cerebros están llenos.

En resumen,

uno solo necesita . . .

1. Concentrarse mucho.

2. Extender las alas.

3. Aletear.

¡Es facílisimo!

Max y el Pájaro se concentran mucho.

Extienden sus *alas* . . .

Y aletean.

No pasa nada.

Aletean por la mañana.

Nada de nada.

Aletean por la tarde.

Nada en absoluto.

Aletean por la noche.

Nada.

Max y el Pájaro están cansados.
Duermen toda la noche.

Y toda la noche sueñan que vuelan.

Al día siguiente, con la cabeza llena de sueños,
Max y el Pájaro vuelven a probarlo . . .

Aletean
y aletean
hasta quedar doloridos.

Nada de
NADA.

El Pájaro aletea, patalea, y GRITA:

¡ESTO NO ES DIVERTIDO! ¡ME ABURRO, ME ABURRO ME ABURRO!

¡Aletear
no funciona!

"Tranquilo", dice Max. "Le pediremos a alguien que
sepa volar que nos diga cómo tenemos que hacerlo".

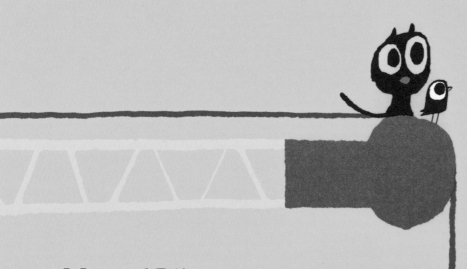

Max y el Pájaro preguntan
(muy educadamente) a la Paloma:
"Disculpe, *si es tan amable,*
¿nos podría explicar
cómo se vuela . . . ,

por favor?

"¡Ja, ja!", cacarea la Paloma
(groseramente).
"¡Mira que no saber volar!
¡Si es MUY fácil!
Solo hay que extender las alas.
Y aletear.

Así . . ."

La Paloma aletea.

La Paloma vuela del revés.

La Paloma vuela en zigzag.

La Paloma hace un rizo.

La Paloma desaparece.

Con una voluntad de hierro, Max y el Pájaro
prueban de nuevo.
Aletean, aletean . . .

. . . y aletean.

Y por la tarde, exactamente a las 5.23,
ocurre algo increíble . . .

De una manera un poco insegura,
¡el Pájaro levanta el vuelo durante 1, 2, 3 segundos!

¡VIVAAAA!

¡Lo hemos conseguido!

"Gracias por enseñarme a volar",
dice el Pájaro.

"Para eso están los amigos", contesta Max.

"Bueno, un trato es un trato", dice el Pájaro.
"Supongo que ahora me querrás comer, ¿verdad?".

"Oh", dice Max,
"Un aperitivo suculento . . .

Me había olvidado de eso.
Deja que lo piense".

Max empieza a pensar . . .

(Reflexiona mucho.)

"No quiero comerte", dice Max.

"Eso los amigos no lo hacen . . ."

Pero ¿me dejas mirar cómo vuelas, Pájaro?"

"¡SÍ!", dice el Pájaro.

Y realiza su primer rizo.

para

David y Jan

Título original: MAX AND BIRD
Publicado originalmente por Penguin Books Ltd, 80 Strand, Londres WC2R 0RL, Reino Unido
Copyright de texto e ilustraciones © Ed Vere, 2016

de la traducción española:
© EDITORIAL JUVENTUD, S. A., 2017
Provença, 101 - 08029 Barcelona
info@editorialjuventud.es
www.editorialjuventud.es
Traducción de Elodie Bourgeois

Primera edición, 2017

ISBN 978-84-261-4415-7

DL B 1271-2017
Núm. de edición de E. J.: 13.390

Printed in China